ANGELIQUE: BOOK THREE

AUTUMN ALONE

CORA TAYLOR

**Look for the other Angelique stories
in Our Canadian Girl**

Book One: Buffalo Hunt

Book Two: The Long Way Home

ANGELIQUE: BOOK THREE

AUTUMN ALONE

CORA TAYLOR

PENGUIN
CANADA

PENGUIN CANADA

Published by the Penguin Group

Penguin Group (Canada), 90 Eglinton Avenue East, Suite 700, Toronto, Ontario, Canada M4P 2Y3
(a division of Pearson Penguin Canada Inc.)

Penguin Group (USA) Inc., 375 Hudson Street, New York, New York 10014, U.S.A.
Penguin Books Ltd, 80 Strand, London WC2R 0RL, England
Penguin Ireland, 25 St Stephen's Green, Dublin 2, Ireland (a division of Penguin Books Ltd)
Penguin Group (Australia), 250 Camberwell Road, Camberwell, Victoria 3124, Australia
(a division of Pearson Australia Group Pty Ltd)
Penguin Books India Pvt Ltd, 11 Community Centre, Panchsheel Park, New Delhi – 110 017, India
Penguin Group (NZ), cnr Airborne and Rosedale Roads, Albany, Auckland 1310, New Zealand
(a division of Pearson New Zealand Ltd)
Penguin Books (South Africa) (Pty) Ltd, 24 Sturdee Avenue, Rosebank, Johannesburg 2196,
South Africa

Penguin Books Ltd, Registered Offices: 80 Strand, London WC2R 0RL, England

First published 2005

1 2 3 4 5 6 7 8 9 10   (WEB)

Copyright © Cora Taylor, 2005
Full-page illustrations © Greg Banning, 2005
Chapter-opening illustrations © Janet Wilson, 2005
Design: Matthews Communications Design Inc.
Map copyright © Sharon Matthews

Manufactured in Canada.

LIBRARY AND ARCHIVES CANADA CATALOGUING IN PUBLICATION

Taylor, Cora, 1936–
Angelique : autumn alone / Cora Taylor.

(Our Canadian girl)
"Angelique: book three".
ISBN 0-14-305008-7

1. Métis—Juvenile fiction. I. Title. II. Title: Autumn alone. III. Series.

PS8589.A883A839 2005   jC813'.54   C2005-902906-4

Visit the Penguin Group (Canada) website at **www.penguin.ca**

This book is dedicated to my friends
Wilma Fisher Gossen and Omer Ranger,
who are descendants of the original
Angelique Dumas of Batoche,
and to my granddaughters,
Adrienne Livingston and Emily Thomas.

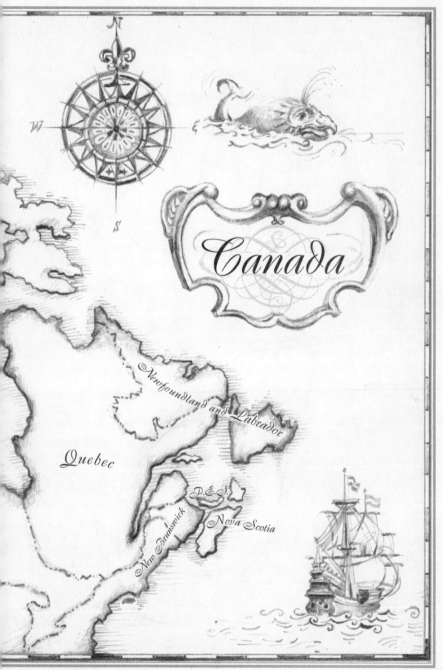

Canada

W   N   S

Newfoundland and Labrador

Quebec

P.E.I.

New Brunswick

Nova Scotia

 Marks the location of the story

ANGELIQUE'S STORY CONTINUES

A LTHOUGH LAND OWNERSHIP along the river in the Batoche area was not recorded until 1873, the Metis in the Saint-Laurent and Batoche area of Saskatchewan had begun to settle there in the early 1860s, trading their nomadic lifestyle for a more permanent one.

Unfortunately, when the Metis began to record their plots of land, no official ownership existed, since the procedures for land ownership in what was then the North-Western Territories had not been set up. The Metis settlers at the time of this story were considered squatters on the land, though as soon as they were able (in 1883), they drew up formal listings and titles to the land.

In the Saint-Laurent and Batoche area, the system of land division was the same as the Metis had used in the Red River area: narrow strips of land that gave settlers the advantage of access to both river and roadway.

There they broke a few acres of land and began growing potatoes and barley. Few raised cattle, preferring to hunt and fish—and of course, the semi-annual buffalo hunts were still a major part of the economy.

In 1867, according to author George Woodcock, "the Hudson's Bay Company sold Rupert's Land to the new Dominion of Canada without consulting any of its inhabitants, Indian, Metis or white." The government immediately set about surveying and allotting the land without regard to the current occupants. This resulted in the Red River Rebellion and would later explode in Batoche in 1885 as the Northwest or Riel Rebellion.

Angelique and her family are among the earliest settlers, although there are records of Metis inhabitants and a fur trade crossing the area as early as 1815.

Author's note: Although most of the characters in this book are fictional, I have, as often as possible, used the surnames of people who were instrumental in settling the area. The real characters of Madeleine and Gabriel Dumont have been portrayed, I hope, as factually as possible and with the greatest respect for the truly amazing people they were.

For translations of Michif words and phrases, see the section called Notes at the end of the book.

Angelique felt like a princess. Even the bride had complimented her.

She shut her eyes and ran her fingers gently down the smooth satin of her blouse. *Could anything be better than the feel of that?* she wondered. She wasn't sure. But when she opened her eyes and saw the deep blue glow of the fabric as it rippled and gleamed in the sunlight, she thought that perhaps the look of it was almost as special as the feel of it.

The bride was her cousin Thérèse. Angelique thought she looked very beautiful in her navy dress with the pink lace that spilled around her neck and cascaded down the bodice of the dress. Thérèse, Angelique knew, had worked very hard making that lace. She was an expert with the bobbin even at her young age—she'd learned from the French nuns at the convent school in St. Boniface where she'd gone last year. Angelique knew that some of the local girls were jealous.

"She'll soon find her hands are too coarse from washing and scrubbing to do such fine work. She'll be sorry, that one!" they said.

But just now, Thérèse's hands looked soft and it appeared her young bridegroom would not let go of the one he was holding as they greeted the people outside the mission church in Batoche.

Angelique looked over at her mother and beamed. Maman was talking to Madame LaVallée. Her mother was smiling, but it was a tired smile. Her face was drawn, and the smile didn't seem to reach her eyes.

Angelique felt a little guilty. She was probably the cause of that tired look. Maman must have been sewing all night to have the blouse ready for her this morning. She couldn't have made it earlier—there weren't that many places in their little cabin to hide things. Angelique had helped Maman sort and tidy all the chests and shelves only this week, and there had been no sign of the blouse. And no satin cloth among the sewing things or anywhere else. The only material cut up for sewing was some heavy flannel cloth that looked to be for a man's shirt. Something for Papa, Angelique supposed. Maman nodded to her and Angelique moved over to stand beside the two women.

Madame LaVallée spoke first. "So, *ma belle,* Angelique," she smiled, "your maman tells me that you are very happy with your new blouse."

Angelique stroked the shimmering cloth of her sleeve and nodded. "*Oui.* I love it. I cannot thank Maman enough for such a wonderful gift."

"Ah," said her mother. For a moment a twinkling smile lit her tired eyes. "But you must thank Madame LaVallée also." She waited long enough to see Angelique's puzzled look and said, "You see, *she* made it!"

Angelique couldn't say anything. She looked from one woman to the other and shook her head.

"It is true, *ma petite*," her mother laughed. "I knew that I could never hide it from you or have time enough to sew it before your birthday and the wedding, and so we traded."

Angelique still shook her head, disbelieving.

Madame LaVallée smiled. "That's right. Your maman is sewing a shirt for my husband and I did your blouse."

Angelique beamed at Madame LaVallée. Now she was grateful to the kind woman not only for her beautiful blouse but also because she no longer felt guilty that her mother looked so tired today.

"Thank you. It is beautiful!" Her birthday had been yesterday, but the real celebration was to be able to wear her new blouse on such a special occasion. She held her arm up to her face to

allow the satin to caress her skin. "It is so soft …
like a baby's cheek!"

She felt silly then. Had she made too much fuss
over the blouse? She caught Madame LaVallée
giving her mother a look and was grateful that
Joseph came rushing over.

"Come quickly, Angelique. Papa says we may
walk down to the river and watch the scow
unload." He was pulling at her arm now and she
didn't dare pull back lest he tear her wonderful
blouse. "*Vite,* Angelique!" Once they were away
from their mother, his voice became even more
excited. "Perhaps Monsieur Fisher will even let
us have a ride across!"

Angelique knew that was unlikely. If there were
carts and people to ferry across, he would not
want to have children hanging about—and
Joseph liked to watch the swirling current as they
crossed the river. He would lie on his stomach
with his head over the edge until Monsieur Fisher
yelled at him to move. No, she was sure they
would not be allowed to cross. Still, it was a

beautiful day and the walk would be nice. Maman had said she and Madame LaVallée were going to help spread out the food everyone had brought for the feast after the wedding mass. Already, the men were setting up planks on sawhorses to make tables. The women had brought their best sheets and tablecloths to cover them.

Angelique would have liked to linger outside the church so that the other girls might see her special blouse glistening in the sunlight, but there would be time for that later. Besides, she caught Father Moulin watching her and was afraid he might think she was guilty of the sin of Pride if she stayed longer, showing off. So she turned to go quietly with her brother.

"Angelique!" Father Moulin was calling her. Oh, no! Had she really been too vain about the blouse? Somehow it seemed to lose some of its special glow as she moved over, head down, to stand in front of him.

"You know that I will commence teaching the children again at the mission in a week or two.

Joseph will be coming as well, so I am counting on you to set a good example."

Relief flooded over her—it was not to be a lecture in front of everyone after all. She nodded meekly. *"Oui, mon Père. J'essayerai."* She was careful to speak clearly and use no Michif words. Father Moulin insisted that his students speak "proper" French.

Angelique's relief at not being in trouble for pride in her new blouse slipped away; now she was worrying about school. She knew there would be hours spent sitting in the hard seats, feeling nervous that when she answered a question, she would be in trouble—not because she did not know the right answer, but because she simply did not say the words correctly. She was glad to see that Father Moulin was calling some of the other children over to tell them the same news.

She could see her friend François LaVallée on the outer ring of the group, but instead of speaking to him, she slipped away to where Joseph still waited, standing on one leg and then the other as he fidgeted with impatience.

"Race you!" he cried and was away running.

"Some race, when you give yourself a head start!" she laughed, but she was off, dashing after him.

They ran until they reached the ridge of the hill overlooking the flats, the place they called Mission Ridge. Then Angelique stopped. She knew she could overtake Joseph, even though he was fast for a six-year-old and getting faster every day. She just did not want to risk falling if she ran down the steep hill. Not only was the road steep, but it was also deeply rutted from the Red River carts that went downhill to cross the river.

Joseph shouted with glee when he noticed and came running back.

"Aha!" he shouted. "Beat you! I guess you can't run so fast now that you are a year older!"

Angelique was about to reply when Joseph's face crumpled into a worried look. "Will that happen to me on my birthday?"

*They ran until they reached
the ridge of the hill overlooking
the flats, the place they
called Mission Ridge.*

Joseph's birthday was only two weeks away and until now he could hardly wait. Angelique could tell that this was something that hadn't occurred to him before. She resisted the temptation to tease him by making him believe that he would run more slowly at seven than he did at six.

"No," she consoled him. "You will be faster than ever."

He was smiling again. "Good," he said, "because Papa said we would be on the hunt for my birthday this year. Maybe I can run with you to find the buffalo Papa has shot."

Angelique stopped in her tracks. She hadn't thought of that—she knew the fall hunt would be coming soon, but the men hadn't spoken of the exact time. It was wonderful news! She loved the excitement of the hunt, especially the feasting and dancing afterward. She would try to be even more help to Maman than she had been the last time. Perhaps then Maman would not look so tired. Angelique smiled at Joseph. Père Moulin must not have known it was time for the hunt.

Most of the children from Batoche, Saint-Laurent, and La Petite Ville would be going. He would have to start later or have his classes with only the unlucky ones who had to stay behind.

To Angelique the sun shone brighter again and her blouse glowed even more vividly in its beams.

"Come, Joseph, when we reach the level ground, I will show you how much faster I can run now that I am eleven!"

Things were not going well. Angelique had been looking forward to visiting the East Village of Batoche with Maman and Papa, but everything had gone wrong.

Angelique darted under the tangle of high-bush cranberry and chokecherry bushes, away from the rutted roadway that led down to the ferry landing. Golden poplar leaves littered the ground, crunching beneath her feet. She'd have to stay still to keep from making noise. She was far enough from the road now to flop down and hide.

She knew she wasn't completely hidden—after all, she could see Joseph's legs as he ran down the steep path. But she was counting on the fact that if she couldn't see his head, then he couldn't see hers. He would have to crouch down to see her, and he was going too fast for that.

She'd run away from Joseph because she was tired of getting in trouble when he misbehaved.

It wasn't fair. Maman expected Angelique to look after Joseph, but he wouldn't listen to her at all. Just now he'd deliberately upset the chair Angelique had been about to sit on when he should have been standing quietly waiting for Maman as he'd been told. And Maman hadn't scolded him at all.

"Angelique!" she had said in an angry voice. "Can't you look after your brother for a little while?"

Angelique had wanted to tell Maman that it wasn't her fault, but there was Madame Ross looking cross and Maman looking so tired and upset that all Angelique could do was grab Joseph by the arm and pull him outside.

She got him that far at least but then he began to struggle, and she wasn't about to have a wrestling match with him in front of everyone. She thought she could still win, but it wouldn't be easy. Joseph could kick and scratch like a wildcat when he was angry. So she let go, and when he came after her, she began to run. She could still easily beat him in a race.

Now she lay here amid the wonderful smell of the autumn leaves—poplar leaves mostly, as the berry bushes still had theirs, which was fortunate as it made this a good place to hide.

She watched as Joseph ran by.

Good. She had tricked him. Let him look for her down by the ferry landing; she could hide here a bit longer. She breathed in the sharp smell of the leaves, that wonderful scent of fall that blended with the woodsmoke from the cabins along the river. She could lie here awhile and forget that Maman was angry with her. She wished Maman were not so impatient and worn out these days. In a few more days, they would be leaving for the hunt. Angelique could hardly wait. She thought once more of the excitement and the beauty of watching her father's buffalo runner, Michif, as he raced after the herd, his tail streaming behind.

For a moment, she let herself drift in memories. She had loved the beautiful pinto horse since he was a foal, cared for him when he'd been gored by a buffalo on the last hunt, and, most wonderful of all, ridden him herself. Lying here with her eyes closed, she could remember the feeling, the prairie wind in her face as the horse galloped beneath her so smoothly it felt as if they were flying.

There were voices, people coming up the trail. Joseph would be with them. Now she could creep out and follow him back. Maman would be finished having tea now. Angelique sat up, brushing the leaves from her hair as she searched the people, looking for Joseph. There were children, she recognized the Vennes, but no sign of Joseph.

She scrambled up, looking frantically back down the trail. There had been lots of time for Joseph to have checked the people down by the ferry landing and realized she was not there. He should be coming back to look for her. She fought her way through the tangle of berry bushes, looking frantically down the trail.

No sign of Joseph. What if he had managed to sneak on board the ferry without Monsieur Fisher noticing? He might get off on the Saint-Laurent side of the river and then what would happen to him? She was running now. What if he had fallen overboard? She could see his pale face beneath the water as he was swept away by the current.

Angelique was running so fast that she almost bumped into her friend François, who was standing watching some people trying to coax a team of oxen to board the ferry on their way to Fort Carlton.

"François," she gasped, "have you seen …"

She caught her breath and stood stock-still.

OUR CANADIAN GIRL

There was Joseph standing beside François, looking innocent as a lamb.

"Joseph!" She grabbed her brother by the arm. "You wretched boy!" She began to drag him back. This time he could resist all he wanted— she was not going to get in trouble with Maman again. She would get him back to the Rosses in time if she had to haul him by the ears all the way up the bank.

To her surprise, he hardly struggled at all. It seemed he had decided to vent his anger another way.

"Just for that," he said, "you will have to ride home in the cart with Maman. If you had been nice to me, I would have let you ride Gurnuy with me."

Angelique was not going to be upset by that. She didn't care if she didn't get to ride Joseph's pony; it was better to be away from Joseph altogether. "I don't care if you fly home, so there!"

Joseph looked at her, smiling smugly.

That was puzzling. Normally, he would have been furious and she would have had a terrible time getting him back to Maman. He was up to something, and Angelique didn't like it.

"I know something you don't know," he taunted.

"Not likely." She doubted he had anything up his sleeve to bother her, but if he did, pretending she didn't care was the fastest way to get him to tell.

They had reached the top of the riverbank now, and Angelique could see her mother climbing into the cart in front of the Rosses' cabin. Joseph's pony was tied behind and Papa was looking around impatiently.

"Yes," said Joseph triumphantly as they ran to the cart. "I heard Papa telling Michel Dumas that Maman was not well enough to go on the hunt. And"—he paused triumphantly—"he said that you would be staying behind to look after her!"

"Un bebé!" Angelique could not believe her ears.

Yesterday, when Joseph had dropped his bombshell, she'd been dumbstruck. She'd felt as if the news had been a rock thrown at her chest. It had lain there all the way back to their cabin. She'd been afraid to speak lest she burst into a fit of angry crying. She had been on every hunt since she could remember. Until last year, she'd stayed with the women in the camp and had not really seen much of the hunt itself. But now she was older and could help, and she and Maman would not be going.

Angelique had known Maman was not her usual happy, healthy self. She had been so tired and impatient with them these last few weeks.

But it had not been until this morning, when they were making bannock and her mother had to go and sit while Angelique finished, that she had dared to ask what was wrong.

Un bebé! How could such wonderful news cause such a terrible thing? Angelique was having trouble knowing which feeling to go with. The joy of having a baby around the house—she remembered Joseph toddling about, but she had not been old enough to hold him or help Maman take care of him when he was tiny—was weighing against the disappointment of not being able to go on the hunt.

"Madame LaVallée says I must get more rest," her mother was looking at her now, her brown eyes pleading with Angelique to understand. "And you know how hard we have to work cutting the meat, making pemmican ..." Her voice trailed off.

Angelique nodded. She still couldn't trust herself to speak. Maman was right. If she was tired from just the work of their little cabin and garden, then the hunt would be too much for her.

"And she says that even the trip, bumping along in the Red River cart, would not be good for the *bebé*."

Angelique nodded again. Still not trusting herself to speak, she went to Maman and put her arms around her.

Maman smiled down at her. "And there will not be so much work with just the two of us here. Perhaps if the weather is fine and I am feeling better, we can walk down to the river and have a *picnique* by the water."

"That would be very nice," Angelique murmured.

"Do you know something?" Maman whispered. "I hope the *bebé* is a girl like you."

Angelique pushed away and looked at her mother with delight. A girl! A baby sister! Until this moment she'd thought only of a tiny doll-like creature to play with—this was even better. A baby sister would be much more than a doll. Angelique pictured herself walking hand in hand with a little dark-eyed person, all dressed up for church. Or playing house in the bush in a secret place she had found and furnished with a little bench of logs and a stump for a table. She could teach a baby sister so many things, tell her stories, make her pretty toys. It was wonderful! This time, she gave Maman the biggest hug ever.

When Madame LaVallée arrived to have tea, Angelique was sure Maman was looking better already. She did not wait to be told to take Joseph back outside to play but offered to go.

It was rather funny to see the confused look on Joseph's face when Angelique smiled at him and handed him some of the fresh bannock with sugar on it as a special treat. She'd been glaring at him like a storm cloud ever since he'd dropped his bad news the day before. It was almost worth missing the hunt, she thought, to see the superior look wiped off his face.

She told herself she would explain everything to him, but not just yet. He was much easier to handle when he was puzzled.

CHAPTER N°4

Angelique held the knowledge of the new bebé like a secret treasure to help her get through the next two days. She was determined not to tell Joseph. Sometimes she felt a little mean, because she knew he was completely baffled by the fact that she had not only accepted being left behind with Maman but also actually seemed happy about it. But keeping him perplexed really had worked a miracle—he was so curious that he wanted to keep Angelique friendly and was being completely cooperative.

Sometimes she would even test him, just to see

how far she could go. Like now, when they were loading the cart, along with François, who had come over with his mother to help them prepare for the trip. Papa and Joseph would be sharing the LaVallées' tipi, but they would take their own Red River cart.

"Joseph," she commanded, "run to Maman and see if she wants to send extra bannock for you to eat on the way."

Her young brother gave her a long look, and Angelique braced herself for an argument. Perhaps having François there was enough to make Joseph rebel at last. But he didn't say a word; he just ran back to the cabin as she'd asked.

It was François's turn to look at her in surprise. "What have you done to Joseph?" he laughed. "I've never seen him take orders from you before! Usually you have to coax him or bribe him or at the very least trick him into doing what you want!"

"Ah," Angelique smiled back, "I've got a secret and he's dying to know it."

"It must be a good one." François looked at her quizzically. "I came over here expecting to see a long face because you have to miss the hunt. Instead you are amazingly cheerful."

Angelique looked thoughtfully at François. Should she tell him? She was sure that he wouldn't tell Joseph and she was bursting to share the news with someone. "You see …," she began, but it was too late.

"Angelique," Joseph ran up to her. "Maman wants you. Right now!"

She looked at François and shrugged. Maybe she would have a chance to tell him later. She knew that Joseph was enjoying being able to convey an order to her, so she was careful to ignore him as she headed back to the cabin to see what Maman wanted.

By the time she finished helping Maman prepare more bannock for the trip, François had left with Joseph and Papa. They were driving the cart to Monsieur LaVallée's place further along the river.

"Why don't you surprise Papa and go and bring Michif up from the river pasture to the corral here? That way, he will have him handy when they leave in the morning. You've been a great help and there's time before we have to prepare the evening meal." Maman smiled a tired smile.

Angelique beamed. She had not had much time to spend with Michif since their return from the spring hunt. Michif was one of the hunters' horses that had spent the summer running out across the river in the big pasture at Saint-Laurent. Michif had only just come home so that Papa could begin riding him again, preparing for the hunt.

When she arrived at the field and called his name, she was thrilled to see the beautiful horse toss his head in his usual greeting and come galloping toward her.

"Oh, Michif, *mon buu,*" she laughed, stroking his neck and reaching up to pat him. "You remember me."

He nickered and bunted her with his head. He'd done that ever since he was a foal, though now he nearly knocked her over.

"Easy … easy," she laughed, pushing back. He rested his muzzle on her shoulder, making little whickering sounds of pleasure.

"Remember how we flew across the prairie and you were faster than the wind? Much, much faster than the Sioux horses chasing us?"

Michif pulled back his head and looked at her. It was as if he were nodding that he understood, Angelique thought.

"And soon you will be racing after the buffalo again," she said as she stroked his side, running her fingers around his white and bay pinto patches. "Look, I can hardly see the scar where the buffalo gored you. You saved my life that day too."

She moved back to scratch behind his ears, her face serious now. "You must be brave again and carry Papa safely." Angelique let Michif blow his breath against her cheek. She could not speak now. She must not let Michif know she had heard Papa talking with the men, wondering if the encounter with the buffalo cow that had gored the pinto would make Michif useless as a buffalo runner this time.

Angelique couldn't bear to think of that, and she didn't want the horse to sense her worry. She must think of something else.

She shut her eyes and said a little prayer that Michif would carry Papa safely and well and be successful in the hunt. Perhaps she could offer up her sacrifice of missing the hunt with her prayers at the mission church. That was it—she would be cheerful and help Maman and not feel sorry for herself. But Michif was still looking as if he sensed her worry; he was tossing his head and acting nervous.

Suddenly a smile lit up her face. A perfect solution.

"You must be brave, *mon buu* Michif," she beamed, "and I will tell you a beautiful secret!"

CHAPTER N°. 5

The carts began to leave well before daybreak. The nice thing about the spring hunt had been that then the days were getting longer; now the darkness came earlier and lasted longer. The nights were cooler too, with a hint of frost in the air. Soon the buffalo would be heading south to their winter pasture. If the hunters hurried, they could find the herds easily.

Papa had ridden out in the dawn half-light, ahead of the carts. He would be joining *le grand* Gabriel and the other hunters, riding ahead to look for a good camping place and scout for signs of the buffalo herds.

Angelique had been up early too. Papa had let her take Michif for a drink. She had pumped some water into the trough, and while he was drinking, she'd petted and talked to him.

"You will go like the wind, *mon buu* Michif, and carry Papa the way you did when I rode you, and you will be very brave and help Papa shoot us two fine buffalo, just as you did last spring. Two buffalo with good hides to trade at the store ... and," she laughed as he finished drinking and raised his head, dribbling water all down her shoulder as he nuzzled her, "you will not tell Joseph our beautiful secret!"

Joseph and his pony had stayed the night with the LaVallées. François's aunt was driving their Red River cart. Joseph and François would be riding their ponies, staying close so that Madame LaVallée could keep an eye on them. All morning, the dust rose on the road running past Angelique's house as carts and riders passed by.

The people from Saint-Laurent were crossing

the river, so their carts and riders had joined the procession as well. They would move on to collect the Metis families from La Petite Ville. It was amazing that the slow-moving carts could raise so much dust, but they did.

Through the dust Angelique could see Thérèse and her new husband pass by in their Red River cart. It was their first hunt as man and wife, so Alphonse had made the sacrifice of driving the cart instead of riding ahead with the other hunters. Thérèse was smiling happily as she waved to Angelique.

Angelique stood outside until Joseph and François rode by so she could wave to them to prove she was not guilty of the sin of Envy. As soon as they passed, she ran back into the house.

She told herself it was the dust that was making her eyes water.

She wondered if today was too early for Maman to feel well enough for their *picnique*. She wouldn't ask. Maman was resting now. In spite of everyone's help, she had worked hard organizing things yesterday, and this morning she had been up early, smiling goodbye to Papa and Michif.

By late morning the last cart had gone by. Suddenly, the day was still. No more screeching carts or people laughing and calling to each other. Silence. For the first time since dawn, Angelique could hear the birds call from the bushes along the river.

It seemed that everyone but Angelique and Maman had gone on the hunt. The farms around them were deserted. Angelique had no trouble knowing that. The way the Metis were dividing the land, in long strips leading down to the river so that each property had access to the trail and to the river, meant that the houses were only a short walk apart.

Usually, there were dogs barking and voices drifting along from the homes on either side. Now all was silent. Even the dogs had gone on the hunt.

There was nothing to do in the house, and Angelique did not want to make noise and disturb Maman's rest. She had washed the dishes that were left from Papa's hurried breakfast. Perhaps she would take a pail and go pick some cranberries along the riverbank. Maman would be pleased if she did that. They had already dried Saskatoon berries to add to the pemmican that would be made during the hunt.

Even if the day was lonely, Angelique wanted to make it last as long as she could. Tomorrow, Father Moulin's classes were beginning. She had hoped they would be postponed until the other children returned from the hunt, but instead he had announced in church yesterday that he would begin teaching right away. Those who could come would be getting "extra" help. She was not looking forward to that.

She had just picked up the berry pail when her mother called from the big bedroom. The cabin was small, only three rooms. In the big front room, they cooked, ate, and sat to visit when company came. There were two rocking chairs covered with bearskin where Papa and Maman sat, and there was a cot covered in striped

Hudson's Bay blankets. That was where Joseph slept now. Before, he and Angelique had shared the small bedroom, but Maman had decided last month that he should move out.

At the time, Angelique had thought it was because she was getting older or maybe just because they fought too much. Now she realized it was because she would be sharing the room with the *bebé*. The thought made her hug herself with happiness.

"Yes, Maman." She hurried to the bedroom doorway. Perhaps she would not pick berries at all; perhaps she would clear a place for the *bebé*. Perhaps Maman would let her bring in Joseph's cradle from the lean-to behind the cabin where it was piled under other things they didn't use. She smiled happily, imagining herself lying in bed looking over at the cradle with a beautiful *bebé* girl lying there smiling at her. *"Une petite ange,"* she murmured to herself.

"Pardon?" her mother was looking at her, puzzled. Then she laughed. "Ah, your head is in the sky again, gathering clouds, is it?" She gave Angelique a little hug. "I think we could prepare *un petit dejeuner* to eat beside the river, don't you?"

Angelique was overjoyed. Surprised too—Maman still looked very pale and tired, even after resting all morning.

"You have been such a good help to me, and I know you are sad not to go on the hunt with Joseph and Papa. So I think you deserve a treat. Run and fetch an onion ... a big one to slice."

Last week Angelique had helped Maman braid all the onions they had pulled from the garden. They hung from the rafters of the cabin at the kitchen end. She climbed on a stool and cut one down now. While Maman sliced the bread and onion, Angelique moved to the other end of the table to do the buttering; she wanted to be as far as possible from the smell of the fresh-cut onion. Maman already had tears streaming down her cheeks. But the sandwiches would be good.

Angelique had made the butter thick and Maman would put lots of salt on the onions. It was what they always had when they took their walks by the river.

Just when this day had been going well, everything went horribly wrong. Angelique stood outside the mission. Classes were over and she had been about to walk home when Pelagie Dumont had come over to talk to her. She tried to tell herself Pelagie had meant no harm, but that didn't help.

"So your maman must be very ill that you cannot go on the hunt," Pelagie said sympathetically.

Angelique knew that Pelagie had stayed behind with her grandmother when her family had left for the hunt. "Maman is just a little tired and …"

"I know," Pelagie interrupted, full of herself at knowing. "Maman said you will be having a little brother or sister."

Angelique was shocked. Everyone must have known but her and Joseph. Of course, she supposed, the women would know and talk among themselves. Pelagie had probably found out that way. She tried not to think that Pelagie might have known before Angelique herself did.

Quickly she recovered and smiled. "Yes, we are very happy."

"But," Pelagie insisted, "there must be something wrong. Women carrying babies go on the hunt all the time. Remember last spring? Evangeline Larocque had her baby while they were there."

Angelique had forgotten about that. She felt as if Pelagie had stuck a knife in her heart. She should have realized there was more to it than just being tired and being with child—Maman was really ill. Yesterday on the way back from their *picnique,* she had stopped suddenly as they climbed the bank and had to sit awhile. She had complained that her back was hurting, and Angelique had been worried at first to see her mother flinch as if she was stabbed with pain. But after a little while, Maman had risen and apologized for spoiling their little walk. Now Angelique remembered how Maman had leaned on her as they'd walked the rest of the way, her face drawn and her jaw clenched.

When Angelique had left for school this morning, Maman had gone back to bed, walking slowly, holding her back. Angelique didn't even stop to say goodbye to Pelagie. She started to run.

She had barely taken three steps when Father Moulin called her.

"Angelique!"

Reluctantly, Angelique turned and ran back.

"I want to commend you on a good day's work," he smiled. "Your answers were very good. You have the makings of an excellent student."

Angelique had tried very hard all day. She had been very careful to keep her answers to his questions short so she did not risk saying the words the Michif way or using any Cree words. It was kind of Father to praise her, but all she wanted to do was get home to Maman.

"Maarsi," she said, bowing her head politely.

The moment the word left her lips she realized her mistake. In her hurry she had said it the Michif way instead of saying *"merci"* as the French did. Angelique clapped her hand over her mouth but it was too late. Father Moulin was frowning down at her.

"Come," was all he said and Angelique followed him meekly back into the room.

Silently he took a piece of slate and wrote *"Je dirai toujours 'merci.'"*

"Twenty times," he said sternly.

Angelique knew the procedure. Every student did. You wrote the words on your piece of slate until it was full and then took it to be checked, then erased it and began again. If she wrote small, she could get it on her slate twice. Writing it didn't take the time; what took time was going and standing patiently beside Father Moulin's desk while he stopped reading his book, checked the words, and made a mark of how many times she had written it and how many more she must do. Blinking back tears, Angelique set to work.

She knew that she should not be angry with Father. After all, Maman said he was only trying to see that Angelique could read and write and speak French properly. She knew Maman was proud that her daughter was learning to read and write, something Maman had not been taught. Papa said that she could learn to speak French at school and still speak Michif with them at home. Many people spoke even more than two languages, he said.

"Look at *le grand* Gabriel. He speaks Cree, Sarcee, Blackfoot, even a bit of Sioux as well as Michif *and* French."

"And," added Maman, "his wife, Madeleine, even speaks English."

That didn't help Angelique now. All she could do was worry about Maman. What if the pain was worse? There were no neighbours nearby to help. Angelique wrote the words as carefully and quickly as she could.

CHAPTER N°. 7

Angelique was out of breath by the time she reached the cabin. Her side hurt from running such a long way, but she had just held it and kept going. She pulled open the door and rushed in.

"Maman!" she called.

She stood listening, trying to hold her breath so that her panting would not drown out any answer. All she could hear was the beating of her heart.

She ran to the bedroom doorway and pulled aside the blanket that covered it. Slowly she let out her breath in a sigh of relief. Maman was sleeping.

Angelique felt foolish. Once again, she had let her imagination cause her to worry needlessly and come rushing in shouting. She might have disturbed Maman's nap.

Strange, she thought—*Maman has not wakened.* Papa always joked that Maman slept so lightly that a mouse tiptoeing across the kitchen floor would waken her.

"Sorry for the noise, Maman." Angelique went over to the bed and put her hand gently on her mother's shoulder. There was no response.

"Maman!" Angelique was afraid now. She wanted to grab her mother and shake her awake. The terrible stillness frightened her. She noticed a large bruise and swelling on her mother's forehead just at the hairline. Something had happened; Maman was hurt.

What she would have done if at that moment her mother had not moaned and moved a little, Angelique did not know.

Angelique went over to the
bed and put her hand gently
on her mother's shoulder.
There was no response.

"Maman!" she flung herself on the bed sobbing with relief. "Maman … say something!"

Her mother's eyelids flickered. Angelique knew she was trying to speak.

"Angelique …"

Angelique put her cheek closer to her mother's lips.

"*Oui*, Maman …"

"Get"—the voice was stronger now—"get Madame LaVallée …"

Angelique was so pleased she had been able to understand what Maman was trying to say that it took her a moment to realize her mother had forgotten that the LaVallées had all gone on the hunt. There was nobody at the farm next to them. Or the one after that. In fact, it had been strange walking all the way to the mission this morning and seeing no one along the way.

"But … Maman …," she started to explain, to remind her mother. Then she realized that Maman's eyes were closed again.

Angelique stood up. Maman was right, she

must get help. Just because Maman was too sick to remember that the LaVallées were not at home didn't change that.

Where could she go? There was no point in running back to the mission; Father Moulin had left when she had, going to cross the river to visit someone at Saint-Laurent. He would be gone by now.

She could go beyond Mission Ridge, down the slope to the river to try to find someone at the top of the bank, but that was much farther, almost a mile. Would there be anyone there?

She could go the other way and hope that it would not be too far before she found someone still at home. Angelique knew that Madeleine Dumont had not accompanied her husband on the hunt. She was looking after someone who was not well enough to go. But their farm by Gabriel's Crossing was nearly six miles down the river. She must find someone nearer than that.

She ran out the door. Pelagie and her *grandmere* were not too far away. Pelagie's grandmother might not be well enough to come, but they would at least be able to tell Angelique if there was someone else near them.

She was out on the road now. She had hoped that there might be someone coming, but a quick glance down the road to the mission told her that there was no one that way. No one ahead either as she began to run toward Pelagie's.

Those few minutes at home had been good for one thing. She could run again. She vowed she would run until she dropped, stitch in her side or not.

Two more plots of land, two more empty cabins, and then she was turning down the roadway to Pelagie's.

The Dumonts' cabin was bigger than Angelique's. Pelagie's father, Isadore, had put on an extra room when his mother came to stay with them. There were chickens pecking and scratching about the yard that ran away squawking as Angelique neared. That was not the only alarm sounded; the Dumonts' old dog came barking around the cabin, but Angelique did not even slow to pet him before she was pounding on the cabin door. She could see Pelagie's face in the window, looking worried. Then Pelagie realized who it was.

Angelique hardly waited for the door to open before she pushed in, throwing Pelagie off balance. The grandmother was sitting in the rocking chair and knitting. She looked much frailer than Angelique remembered. Sadly, she realized that there would be no help for Maman here.

"Maman is hurt, Pelagie!" she said breathlessly. "Is there anyone nearby who can help?"

"Not close by." Pelagie shook her head. "*Tante* Madeleine would be the best help, but she is far away."

Angelique turned to leave. It was hopeless; all she could do was return home and pray that someone came by on the trail from the river. Then, through the window, she saw a black horse behind the house in a corral. She had an idea. "Is that your horse?"

Again Pelagie shook her head. "It is a new one Papa just got. I don't ride horses."

Angelique remembered. She had overheard Pelagie telling one of the Letendre girls after church that she did not think riding horses was "ladylike." For a moment, Angelique had hoped that Pelagie could ride to her aunt's while Angelique went home to stay with Maman. Every moment away from her, wondering how she was faring, was torture. Now that hope was dashed.

"You are welcome to take it though," Pelagie said, then she looked worried. "Except, I heard Papa say it was only 'green broke.' I know you are a good rider but …"

Everyone knew of Angelique's ride on Michif after the spring hunt, when horse raiders had stolen him and many of the other Metis horses. Angelique, François, and Joseph had rescued the horse. She knew people still talked about it. Some would smile at her and tell her she was very brave. Others called her "foolhardy" and "wild," though they did not say it to her face.

"Green broke" meant that a horse had learned to wear a halter or bridle and saddle but that it had not been ridden. Or had been ridden very little. It would probably buck the minute someone got on its back.

It seemed to Angelique that she had no choice. "Come," she said, trying to sound confident. "Would you help me get a bridle on it?"

CHAPTER *N°* 8

The horse was a lot smaller than Michif.
It was probably a two-year-old, Angelique
decided, which would be why it hadn't yet been
broken to ride.

"Come, Mennwi," Pelagie called.

Her voice was quivering, and Angelique was sure
the horse would sense her nervousness and be even
harder to catch. They had found a bridle and even-
tually a saddle that had seen better days. Obviously
the good saddles had been taken for the hunt.

"Mennwi," she called, moving in front of
Pelagie to reach through the rails of the corral.

"Good, Mennwi … that is a good name for such a beautiful horse." She held a handful of grass she'd pulled.

Mennwi was not as fine a horse as Michif but his coat gleamed in the sunlight. Angelique would have liked to take her time getting to know him, but she couldn't spare even a minute now. Carefully she climbed over the rails, talking calmly, trying to lure Mennwi toward her.

He came more quickly than she had hoped. He was wearing a halter and she reached behind her to where she'd looped the halter shank on the rail. While he sniffed at and started to eat the grass from her hand, she quickly attached the rope and moved back so that she could jump onto the rails if Mennwi panicked once he realized he was tied.

She was glad she had not left it up to Pelagie to hand her the halter shank. Pelagie had backed away from the fence, eyes wide with fear. So much for getting help putting on the saddle.

"Pelagie!" she spoke softly so as not to alarm the horse, even though she would have liked to yell the command. "Bring me some more grass!

Mennwi discovered he was tied, but to Angelique's relief he did not fight the rope. Obviously that part of his training had progressed. She fed him the grass Pelagie brought, stroking him as she did so. He trembled but stood still.

"*Bon* Mennwi." Again she would have liked to take some time but there was none. When he was almost finished chewing the grass, she slipped the bit into his mouth and pulled the bridle on over his ears. She worked quickly to fasten it. She realized she would have to leave the halter on—she would need him tied when she put the saddle on him. She would prefer to ride without a saddle as she did when she rode Michif, but if Mennwi bucked, she'd need one.

She'd hung the saddle over the top rail of the corral. Now she moved toward Mennwi, holding it out for him to smell. He snorted and shook his head but just backed away a little.

Grateful that the horse was not as tall as Michif, Angelique threw the saddle on his back.

Again he shook and danced a little before snorting and standing still. Now she had to reach under his belly to get the cinch.

For the first time, she was afraid, afraid of being kicked. Then she remembered Maman lying back at the cabin, alone and so still. That thought was all she needed to give her courage.

"Good Mennwi, good horse … stand!" And he did.

She took a deep breath and slipped beneath the trembling horse. A moment was all it took.

She tightened the cinch, waited a minute until the horse breathed out at last and hitched it tight again. There! The saddle was on. She looked around. Thank goodness, Pelagie was still there.

"Now, Pelagie!" she said, keeping her voice calm so that Mennwi would think she was still speaking to him. "When I am in the saddle, quickly undo the halter shank from the halter. Then once I am riding Mennwi, open the corral gate so that we can leave."

Angelique kept her hands on the rope under Mennwi's chin and waited until Pelagie was at the rail. Then she put her foot in the stirrup and leapt into the saddle.

CHAPTER N° 9

For several seconds the horse stood still.
Angelique could feel him shaking beneath her.
Then it was as if he decided to take flight.
Straight up.

Angelique's head snapped back as the horse
came down. She had time only to be sure that
she had a good hold of the saddle in her right
hand before he was off again, bucking his way
around the corral.

She hung on, her head flying back and forth
like a rag doll's. *How long can I do this before I am
thrown off or the cinch breaks?* she wondered. *How*

long will Mennwi keep bucking?

This time when her head straightened, Angelique could see Pelagie running. To Angelique's horror, the girl was opening the corral gate.

"Not yet!" Angelique screamed, but she could hardly hear herself. It was too late anyway.

Mennwi had seen the gate opening too. It stopped his bucking but now he was going at a dead gallop across the corral, through the narrow space, out into the yard, and down the road.

To Angelique's amazement, she was still on his back. Even more astonishing, she had somehow managed to hold on to the reins in her left hand, even though it too was tightly clamped to the saddle. She crouched forward, pulling on the reins. She had to gather them enough to turn him to the right when they came to the road. Could she do it?

She didn't have to. Mennwi turned and raced along the road. This was hardly the wonderful flying feeling she'd had when she rode Michif, but at least she was still on the horse's back, not lying in a crumpled heap back at the corral.

The good news was that since she was heading in the right direction, she could let Mennwi have his head as long as he wanted to race. And at this speed they would get to Madeleine Dumont faster than Angelique had dreamed.

But, she wondered, would she be able to slow him and turn him when she needed to?

She closed her eyes against the wind; they were watering so much she could hardly see anyway. All she had to do was stay on Mennwi's back for now.

They met no one. At last Mennwi slowed to a trot and then a walk. Angelique looked down. The horse's sides were lathered with sweat. She would have to let him walk for a bit. At least if he was walking, she would have no trouble turning him when they came to the Dumonts' little farm.

Now she had time to think of Maman. Angelique did not know how much time had passed since she'd left her lying there so pale and

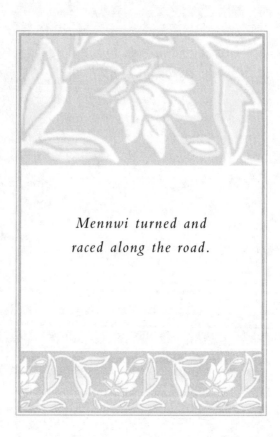

*Mennwi turned and
raced along the road.*

still. It was bad enough that Maman might have trouble having the *bebé* without being injured now too.

Angelique felt ashamed of her selfishness. All she had thought of was herself, enjoying being a proud big sister. She should have known that Maman did not have babies easily. Why else was there only Joseph and her? Everyone else seemed to have big families. François had six younger brothers and sisters. And she should have realized when Maman was always tired and easily upset that she was not well. Normally, Maman had the sweetest nature in the world. The tears that welled up in Angelique's eyes now were not from the wind.

A partridge broke from the long grass beside the trail and Mennwi shied, nearly throwing her, but she held on. It started him going more quickly again, though she managed to keep his head up so that he couldn't buck. He was back at a full gallop now, and she couldn't slow him. She worried once more that he might race right by the Dumonts'.

The newly built house and stable were in sight now. Angelique pulled on the reins as hard as she could, but there was no slowing Mennwi.

What could she do? She considered trying to jump from the horse as it ran by. At least then she could deliver her message.

As quickly as the idea came into her head, she knew it was foolish—she could be killed. The only thing she could do was wait until he tired again, and then she could rein him around and bring him back. More tears came now. That would be such a waste of time. Poor Maman.

But then a miracle happened. Mennwi did slow and without her help, he turned into the farmyard. He trotted straight to the barn. Angelique ducked as he went through the open door and stopped at the manger inside. Angelique couldn't believe it. She jumped off and ran to the house.

She had not noticed that Madame Dumont was in the yard. She came over smiling, but when she saw Angelique's tear-streaked face, she caught her in her arms.

"What is wrong, *ma petite?*" Her face was full of concern. "You are Marguerite Dumas's daughter, are you not? Is she all right?"

Angelique shook her head. For a moment she couldn't speak; the sobs made it difficult for her to say anything. At last all she could say was a muffled, "Help … please come …"

But the good woman was moving already. She had gone to the nearby corral, grabbing a bridle on the way.

Angelique watched as, with quick efficiency, Madeleine Dumont bridled and saddled a horse and led it to Angelique to hold.

"I must quickly tell Madame Doucette that I am going." She ran to the house.

She was back in a few minutes, taking her horse's reins from Angelique. "Get your horse— it went into the barn, did it not?"

Angelique was running to the barn before Madame Dumont had finished speaking. She pulled Mennwi outside the door, trying not to think about what would happen if he bucked

when she tried to mount. Perhaps she could
manage if she did it quickly without thinking or
letting the horse know she was afraid. Her foot
was in the stirrup and she swung herself up
immediately. This time she had a firm grip on the
reins to keep them taut.

She did not know whether it was because she
had made it into the saddle so quickly, or because
Mennwi had grown used to her, or because,
possibly, that he was just tired after his long run,
but to her amazement and relief, he did not
buck, just sidestepped skittishly.

Madeleine Dumont had ridden over beside
her. For the first time she recognized the horse.
"You rode Mennwi here?" There was amazement
tinged with horror in her voice.

Angelique nodded as they began to ride out of
the yard. "Your niece, Pelagie, lent him to me. All
our horses are on the hunt."

The woman had urged her mount into a trot
and Mennwi stayed beside it. Madame Dumont
was shaking her head, a respectful smile on her

face. "You must be an exceptional rider," she said.

"I was afraid," Angelique said, "that I wouldn't be able to slow him to turn in here, but it was like a miracle … When we came to your yard, he turned."

"Not a miracle, little one," the good woman laughed. "We raised Mennwi here and traded him to Isadore. Mennwi was just coming home. It is the second time he's done so." She was urging her horse into a gallop and pulling ahead of Angelique. "The last time," she called back, "he threw my brother-in-law and ran away to come here."

Angelique was worried that Mennwi was too tired to keep pace with the other horse, but the good Madeleine seemed to read her mind. "I am going to ride ahead," she said. "Keep up if you can … otherwise just follow. I want to hurry to your maman. She must be truly ill for you to ride a wild horse to come for help!"

Then Madame Dumont leaned forward and raced ahead, quickly outdistancing Mennwi and Angelique.

Angelique watched in admiration. Obviously, Madame Dumont did not share her niece's opinion that it was unladylike to ride. Not only could Madeleine Dumont read *and* write, but she rode like an expert.

CHAPTER № 10

Angelique decided she would let Mennwi choose whether she rode directly home and returned the horse later or whether she would take him back now and run the rest of the way. She was too worried about Maman to waste time struggling to ride past Pelagie's if Mennwi did not want to go. But they galloped past his new home and he turned obediently when she reined him into her own yard. It took only a matter of seconds to put Mennwi in their corral, slip off the bridle and saddle, and run to the house.

"Maman! Maman!" she called.

The kitchen was empty, but when Angelique rushed to the bedroom doorway and pulled the blanket curtain aside, she could see Madame Dumont bending over the bed. Maman was propped up with pillows, holding a cloth to her head.

Angelique nearly burst into tears again, she was so relieved. It was so good to see Maman awake. "What happened?" she asked.

"Your mother had a dizzy spell and fell against the stove," Madame Dumont explained. "Thank *le bon Dieu* it was a warm day and there was no fire burning."

"It's true," Angelique's mother said. "It was some time before I came to and was able to crawl into the bedroom ... I think I fainted several times on the way ..."

She was smiling but her voice was very weak. "Madame Dumont told me how brave you were to ride for help," she said softly.

Angelique blinked back her tears. "You rest now, Maman," she said. "I will light the fire and make some tea for you both." She turned quickly so Maman would not see her struggling not to cry.

It was good that it took her a while to light the fire and get the kettle boiling. It gave her time to compose herself. It would not do Maman any good to have a daughter crying about the house. She had to be cheerful and not add to her mother's problems by causing worry.

She was just spooning the tea into the pot when she felt an arm around her shoulders.

"Your maman is very fortunate to have a daughter like you."

Madame Dumont was smiling at her, but there was sadness in her smile too. Angelique had heard that Madeleine and Gabriel had been unable to have any children of their own. So they cared for each other more than many couples, and any child they met was made to feel special.

"Merci." Angelique was wondering what else to say when there was a pounding on the door. She rushed to open it.

It was Pelagie, her face red from running. When she saw her aunt she stood very still and looked relieved.

"I saw," she panted, "Angelique ride by on Mennwi and *Mamere* said I should come and see if you were all right … I didn't see you go by, Tante Madeleine."

"Ah, Pelagie. I went by first. Angelique's maman is resting now."

Pelagie smiled. "So she is not going to lose the baby?"

To Angelique's amazement, she had forgotten about the *bebé*. She had imagined coming back to find Maman still unconscious. She had almost left Mennwi's bridle and saddle on in case she had to ride for Père Moulin to come and give her mother last rites. Her fear of losing Maman had made her forget the baby. But now that Pelagie had asked, the answer was terribly important.

Madame Dumont shook her head sadly. "It is hard to say. For now, Angelique's maman must rest and be very careful." She looked at Angelique now. "I know you'll care for her."

Angelique nodded.

"You can walk beside me as far as your home, Pelagie … unless, perhaps, you would like to ride Mennwi?"

The horrified look on Pelagie's face and her aunt's laughter were enough to make Angelique realize that the good woman had been making a joke. It was a relief to laugh after all the worry and tears, and after a moment even Pelagie joined in.

Madame Dumont gave Angelique a hug as they were leaving. "Do you need anything … any food? I could bring something when I come back tomorrow morning."

"No," said Angelique. She had already been planning to make *rababou*. Maman had said that the pemmican left from the last hunt should be used up. It would make a very good stew and there were still potatoes, carrots, and turnips in the garden to add to it. When she and Joseph had helped Maman gather the vegetables to put in the root cellar, they had left a few in the ground so they could eat them fresh right up until the snow fell.

When Angelique stepped outside to watch Pelagie and her aunt leave, she realized it was getting late. Each day it seemed the sun set earlier; the long summer evenings were no more.

Angelique shivered as she thought of how long the winter nights would be. Then she shook herself to shake away such thoughts. Why did she worry about winter nights when this was a perfect fall evening?

She stood for a moment, enjoying the smells of autumn. Overhead a huge flock of geese came in to land on the river below, their honking echoing in the silence. A coyote yelped somewhere on the bank and then another, until their songs filled the evening.

As long as Maman was all right, the terrible day had turned out better than Angelique had hoped it would. She went inside and began to chop the vegetables for the *rababou*.

But when, at last, the stew was ready and she took a bowl of it to Maman, she was disappointed that her mother took only a few bites and waved the food away.

"I'm too tired to eat, *ma petite,*" she apologized. "I will sleep now and eat tomorrow."

Angelique tried to stop her fears. But even though she thought the stew was almost as good as Maman's, she found that her throat didn't seem to want to swallow. She too ate very little.

Tomorrow just had to be a better day. Thank goodness that Madeleine Dumont would come again. For the first time, Angelique wished there were no hunt and that Papa and Joseph were still here.

It turned cold during the night. Angelique woke up shivering and reached sleepily down to pull up the quilt at her feet. Then she remembered Maman and jumped from her cot to run into Maman's room.

Maman's hands were like ice. Angelique spread another cover over her and then decided to add her wool shawl.

Luckily, Papa had made Joseph bring in a good supply of wood, and it took Angelique only a moment to put another stick or two on the coals and blow on the fire to get it going. She lit a candle from the flames and carried it back to Maman.

"Maman?" she said softly. She knew she should let Maman sleep, but Angelique was suddenly afraid to see her lying there so cold and still, even though she could see that Maman was breathing—the covers rose and fell. "Are you all right?"

Her mother's eyelids flickered and opened. "Angelique?"

Now Angelique could see that Maman was shivering worse than she was. Angelique made up her mind. She blew out the candle and set it on the stool beside the bed, pulled back the covers, and climbed in beside her mother. She took those icy hands in her own and pressed them against her face.

For a long time she lay there, pretending she was a stove and could send heat to Maman.

It must have worked because when Angelique woke up at dawn, she lay cuddled in her mother's arms and they were both warm. She savoured the feeling for a minute and then slipped carefully out of bed. She went to add more wood to the stove and heat the kettle for tea. She would, she decided, warm up the stew as well. Maman had hardly eaten all day yesterday, nothing since the tea and bannock she'd had before Angelique had left for the mission school.

Maman was trying to stand up when Angelique returned. She helped her mother use the chamber pot and then took it out to the outhouse to empty while Maman went back to bed. Angelique had arranged all their pillows so that Maman could sit up. She was looking comfortable but exhausted when Angelique got back. The worry must have shown on her face because her mother smiled to reassure her.

"I am feeling much better. Thank you for being my warming rock," she said.

Angelique was relieved to see the smile. She even managed a little laugh at Maman's joke. She knew that her mother was referring to the rocks they heated in the oven and then wrapped in blankets to put in the bed at their feet on cold winter nights. They also used the rocks when they went in the sled in winter. Underneath the buffalo robes they covered themselves with, the heated rocks kept them toasty warm for many a mile.

Maman managed to eat more of the stew this time, dipping some bannock into the gravy and telling Angelique what a *bon opaminawasow* she was.

Angelique was beaming with relief when Madame Dumont arrived.

"Ah," said the kind woman, "it would seem that the patient *and* the nurse had a good night."

Angelique nodded. She would not bother to tell how frightened she had been during the night when she'd felt how cold Maman was.

"Maman," she said, smiling, "has even managed to eat some of my stew for breakfast."

"Wonderful," Madame Dumont said, setting a cloth bag on the table, "and I have brought some griddle cakes for our tea when she is hungry again."

Angelique busied herself fetching some water from the barrel behind the house to put on the stove so that she could wash the breakfast dishes. When the water was warm, she carefully poured in a few drops of the lye soap that stayed melted in the tin on the back of the stove.

As she was drying the dishes, she moved over to the door of Maman's room. It wasn't nice to eavesdrop but she couldn't resist.

She could hear Maman asking the question that Pelagie had asked.

"Do you think I will lose the *bebé*?"

"It is hard to say," Madeleine's voice was gentle. "I am hoping the fall yesterday did not do any harm. Then we will just have to worry about your usual problems."

Angelique could hear her mother's voice replying, but it was so soft that she could not hear what was said. Who would have thought a blanket over the door could block out important sounds? If Angelique got any closer, she'd have to poke her head through. Maman must be facing away. She couldn't stand it.

"Madame," she said pulling the blanket aside. "Would you like some tea?"

Yes, she'd been right. Maman was facing away from the door as Madame Dumont tucked in the bedding on the other side. Angelique wanted to ask about the "usual problems," but she didn't dare. That would be admitting that she'd been eavesdropping. She bit her lip and went to make fresh tea.

"At least you are fortunate in having such a helpful nurse looking after you." Madeleine Dumont's eyes twinkled as she lifted her cup.

Maman smiled. "Yes," she said, "I am well taken care of when Angelique is here. I shall miss her when she goes back to school tomorrow."

Madame Dumont frowned. "I don't think that is wise, Marguerite. We can't have you having another dizzy spell and falling with no one around to help."

Angelique wanted to throw her arms around the kind woman. She was already worrying about leaving Maman alone again, but she knew she'd be sent to school. Maman thought education was very important. Perhaps Madame Dumont could make her see that it was necessary for Angelique to be here.

"It's true, Maman," she said, "and I would not be missing any more than those who've gone on the hunt." She wanted to add that Father Moulin had said she was doing well, but the memory of the lines she'd had to do stopped her.

Madeleine Dumont did not wait for a reply. "Then it's settled," she said firmly as she rose, preparing to leave. "I shall tell Father Moulin Angelique is needed at home until everyone is back from the hunt."

"And," she said softly to Angelique as they stood at the front door, "I want you to keep Mennwi here and not try to take him back to Isadore's. You might need him to come and get me." Then, as if reading the concern on Angelique's face, she added, "It's not likely, *ma petite,* but the horse might as well stay." She laughed and gave

Angelique's shoulder a little squeeze. "There is certainly no chance that Pelagie will be using him!"

Angelique laughed too. She was still smiling as she watched the good woman leave. Then she ran to the pasture to bring Mennwi a couple of carrots she'd pulled from the garden. She might as well stay friends.

CHAPTER N.º *12*

Madeleine Dumont came almost every day, but as the days went by Angelique found that being a nursemaid to Maman was a very lonely job. Her mother seemed to be getting better—at least there were no more dizzy spells, but she slept much of the time, so she wasn't much company. Madame Dumont said that was very good—it was important for Maman to rest, so Angelique was glad. Glad but lonely.

The hunters had been gone for more than a week now, and there had been no word. Indeed, the road past their little farm was very quiet.

Nearly every afternoon, Pelagie would stop by on her way from the mission school to see if Angelique needed anything, and Angelique found herself waiting impatiently for the visits. Not that Pelagie was any fun to play with, but Angelique knew that if there were any news of the hunt, some of the other children at school would have heard. But there was nothing.

The weather was still holding, though Angelique noticed that the nights were growing longer and colder. Frost sparkled on the grass in the morning when she went outside to fetch water from the well for their morning tea. The air was filled with the honking of huge flocks of geese that filled the sky as they came in to land on the river at the foot of their land.

One day Madeleine Dumont brought a freshly killed goose and helped Angelique pluck and clean it. That had been a lot of work but fun too. Angelique couldn't believe one goose could produce so many feathers. Plucking the down was the worst part, but they'd wanted to get as much of it as they could. It would make a lovely warm comforter. For several days afterward, it seemed there were bits of feather everywhere.

Proudly, Angelique had served tender slices of goose to Maman for supper that night.

"What a wonderful treat!"

The best thing of all was seeing Maman's face and her good appetite with the change from their diet of *rababou*.

But most of the time, Angelique's only company was Mennwi. Now he came nickering to her even when she didn't bring him a treat.

One particularly nice day, she dragged Maman's rocker out onto the big step Papa had built in front of the cabin, and Maman sat and rocked. Angelique went to pat Mennwi. Later, she came back to sit at Maman's feet.

"Be careful, Angelique," she teased. "Michif will be jealous when he returns from the hunt! He will think you have forgotten him."

Angelique jumped up indignantly to face her mother. "I wouldn't, Maman! How could you think …" Her words trailed off as she caught the laughing face. "Oh, Maman!"

She was laughing with her mother then. It was wonderful to see Maman feeling so much better. Gone was the pale, tired look. On her last visit, Madame Dumont had predicted there would be no more problems having the baby.

Angelique was just thinking how well things were going when she saw Pelagie running down the road toward them. The girl's face was so serious that they both waited solemnly for her to arrive at the cabin and catch her breath.

"What is wrong, Pelagie?" Maman asked. "Your *grandmere* is not ill, I hope?"

Pelagie was still gasping for breath and couldn't speak.

"It can't be that, Maman," Angelique replied. "She came from the direction of the mission."

"Father Moulin has heard there has been an accident on the hunt," the girl gasped.

Angelique's heart seemed to stop. "Who?" she breathed.

"One of the hunters ... fell ... was killed."
Pelagie burst into a fit of crying.

Angelique wanted to grab her and shake her.
"Who?" She knew she was yelling, but she
couldn't help it.

"Angelique." She felt Maman's arm around
her, holding her, calming her.

How could she be calm? She could see Michif
racing beside the buffalo herd, stumbling and falling and then the herd trampling horse and rider.

"Pelagie," Maman's voice was almost a whisper,
but Angelique could hear the quiet desperation in
it. "It's all right, *ma petite.* Tell us, please."

Pelagie's voice rose to a wail. "No one *knows.*
Father Moulin had a message from Father Andre
but he didn't know ..." She was sobbing louder
now. "Just that it was someone ... not someone
from La Petite Ville ... someone from here!" Her
sobs broke into hiccups, and she buried her face
in Angelique's mother's lap.

"Maman ..." Angelique was crying now too,
though she was trying not to. She must be strong

for Maman. She could feel Maman's fingers gripping her shoulder.

"Someone will come and tell us." Her mother said. "Some of the men will ride ahead and tell the family." She crossed herself. "In the meantime, we must have faith."

Angelique shut her eyes and prayed with all her heart. She could not get the vision out of her mind of the beautiful pinto buffalo runner stumbling and throwing its rider under the stampeding buffalo.

CHAPTER №. 13

Angelique did not open her eyes, even when she heard the sound of hoof beats on the road. She was afraid to look. If it was riders come with the news, she wanted them to ride on by. Let it not be Papa who had fallen. She wished her vision had not been so vivid. She tried to convince herself that it was only her strong imagination "borrowing sorrow" again.

There was only one rider, and the rider did not go by. She felt Maman's grip tighten. When Angelique did turn and look, she recognized Madeleine Dumont's familiar horse as the woman reined into the road to their cabin.

Pelagie got to her feet and Maman did too, but she kept her tight grip on Angelique, as if she dared not let go.

"Is it …?" Maman's voice broke.

"No," Madeleine Dumont said as she dismounted. "At least, I don't know. But I wanted to be here. I knew you would be worried. Here!" she said to Pelagie. "Take the horse and tie it up."

Pelagie looked horrified. Any other time Angelique might have enjoyed the moment. Now she moved away from Maman to help the girl.

"But you must be worried too," Marguerite Dumas protested. "It could be …"

Madeleine Dumont laughed. "It will take more than a herd of buffalo to kill my Gabriel."

Angelique tied the horse without any help from Pelagie. The two girls went back to the cabin to find that Pelagie's aunt had dragged the other rocker out. The two women now sat side by side.

"You two girls can make some tea while we enjoy the sunlight," she said briskly. "This really is a pleasant spot at this time of day, Marguerite."

How wise the woman is, Angelique thought. There would have been no point in insisting her mother go inside and rest.

From where they sat, the two women could watch the road in the direction any rider might come, if that rider was bringing a message from the hunt.

She would have been even more anxious if she hadn't had to keep an eye on Pelagie, whose face crumpled into tears the minute they were in the cabin. Angelique soon discovered that as long as she kept the girl busy, she was all right. Luckily the kettle was not long off the boil, and they soon returned to the porch carrying cups of tea for everyone. Angelique had added a bit of extra sugar to keep up everyone's strength.

The girls had refilled the cups twice when they saw the dust and heard the sound of horses coming. Surely, Angelique thought, Papa would be one of the people riding back with the news—if he were all right. She strained her eyes to see the familiar pinto—her beloved Michif—among the horses she could vaguely discern coming their way. Her heart fell. The horses were all dark, black or bay. Michif was not there. And she could not tell who the riders were.

CHAPTER N.º 14

No one spoke. The women were silent, but Pelagie was sobbing into her hands. Angelique strained her eyes to make out the riders. She recognized the broad shape of Gabriel Dumont.

Then her eyes filled with tears and she began to sob too. The first two riders, Gabriel and one other, were slowing to turn into their road.

Angelique squeezed her eyes tightly shut. She did not want to see. If she could have, she would have closed her ears too. She did not want to hear what the men would have to say. But she could hear all too well—the sound of them slowing to stop in front of the cabin and then nothing but the heavy breathing of the horses that stood snorting before the cabin.

She waited for the men to speak. She would not look at them. Then there was a muffled cry of joy from her mother.

"Louie!"

Angelique's eyes flew open. It was Papa! He was safe and well! Maman was standing, holding her arms out to him. Angelique rushed to share the hug and buried her face in his buckskin jacket. The familiar smell of smoky leather that filled her nostrils seemed better than any flower the prairie could provide. For a long, lovely moment the three of them stayed together.

When at last Angelique looked up, she could see that Madeleine was already mounting her horse. Gabriel stood by with Pelagie, ready to lift her up in front of her aunt.

Angelique was puzzled. They barely waved goodbye before riding out to the main road.

There Madeleine turned back the way the riders had come, taking Pelagie home. Gabriel rode after the other riders, toward the mission.

It was not until Angelique had brought her father and mother more tea that the big question was asked.

"Who was it?" Maman said softly as she stirred her tea.

"Alphonse," he said. His eyes were sad.

Angelique couldn't stop the tears now. Poor Thérèse. She remembered how happy the young bride and groom had been and how merrily Thérèse had waved to her from the Red River cart the morning they had left for the hunt.

Angelique felt she'd been terribly selfish. She had been so worried about Papa, it had not even crossed her mind that if they were spared the tragedy of losing someone they loved, somebody else would be bearing that pain.

She didn't realize at first that Papa was not staying. He would be riding back to join the carts and to bring Thérèse back to stay with them.

For a long, lovely moment the three of them stayed together.

She would look after Maman while Angelique and Joseph went to school at the mission.

Papa fed and watered the strange dark horse before he ate a quick supper with them. It was not until she saw Papa getting ready to leave that Angelique asked the question that had worried her so much. In truth, she had been afraid to hear the answer.

"Michif …?" She couldn't keep the catch out of her voice. "Why didn't you ride Michif back?" The vision of the pinto horse falling among the buffalo flashed through her mind again. Had Michif been afraid to be a brave buffalo runner? She almost hoped it were true—that he had been useless in the hunt—but in her heart, she knew her beautiful Michif would have been as brave as ever.

Papa came and held her, and this time the smell of the buckskin did not comfort her. "I lent him to Alphonse when his horse went lame. I had killed my two buffalo by then," he said, his arms tight around her. "Your Michif ran as well as ever, but there was a gopher hole … and …"

Angelique knew too well what had happened, but she had to listen to the rest.

"He was brave, your Michif. Even though his leg was broken, he got up and stood over Alphonse to protect him. But Alphonse had died from the fall … his neck was broken. And there was nothing to be done for Michif."

Papa's voice broke then, and Angelique didn't want to hear any more. Papa would have had to shoot Michif and that would have been as hard for him to do as it was for her to know.

Through her tears, she watched Papa ride away. Then she turned to go in to Maman. As she did, she glimpsed Mennwi standing just like Michif used to—as if waiting for her. He would have to wait. Maman needed her now. Angelique would also have to help when Thérèse arrived. Poor Thérèse would need all their support and love. It was good that Thérèse would have Maman to take care of now and the *bebé* to help with when it came.

The *bebé*! She had almost forgotten the *bebé*. She shut her eyes and imagined the tiny brown-eyed face smiling up at her.

She would have to be brave, like Michif, she thought as she went to see if Maman needed anything. She was glad she'd told Michif the beautiful secret before he left.

NOTES

The Metis people are descended both from the European fur traders and from the Cree, Ojibwa, and Saulteaux Natives who lived on the Canadian prairies. Their language, called Michif, is a mixture of Cree and French.

I am grateful to Professor Robert A. Papen, Départment de linguistique et de didactique des langues, UQAM, Montreal, for the Michif translations used in the book.

page 55: *mennwi*
Translation: midnight
Note: In French, "midnight" is *minuit*.

page 81: *en bon opaminawasow*
Translation: a good cook
Note: The Michif form of "a" is *en*. *"Bon"* is French for "good," and *opaminawasow* is Cree for "cook."

BIBLIOGRAPHY

Barkwell, Lawrence J., Leah Dorion, and Darren R. Prefontaine. *Resources for Metis Researchers* (Winnipeg: Gabriel Dumont Institute and Manitoba Metis Federation, 1999).

Barnholden, Michael (trans.). *Gabriel Dumont Speaks* (Vancouver: Talonbooks, 1993).

Dobbin, Murray. *The One-and-a-Half Men* (Vancouver: New Star Books, 1981).

Lussier, Antoine S., and D. Bruce Sealey. *The Other Natives: The Metis, Vol. III* (Winnipeg: Manitoba Metis Federation Press and Editions Bois Brules, 1980).

Payment, Diane. *Batoche (1870–1910)* (Saint Boniface, Man.: Les Editions du Ble, 1983).

Payment, Diane. *Les Gens Libres—Otipemisiwak: Batoche, Saskatchewan, 1870–1930: Etudes en archeologie et histoire* (Ottawa: Service des parcs Canada, 1990).

Silver, Alfred. *Lord of the Plains* (New York: Ballantyne Books, 1990).

Van Kirk, Sylvia. *Many Tender Ties* (Winnipeg: Watson & Dwyer, 1993).

Weekes, Mary (as told by Norbert Welsh). *The Last Buffalo Hunter* (Saskatoon: Fifth House, 1994).

Woodcock, George. *Gabriel Dumont: The Metis Chief and His Lost World* (Edmonton: Hurtig Publishers, 1975).

Acknowledgments

Again, special thanks to Professor Robert A. Papen for the Michif translations. I am so grateful to my super editor, Meg Masters. Sorry about the horse, Meg! Thanks too to my researcher, Sean Livingston, and my friend Omer Ranger of Duck Lake for filling in some information about the real Angelique. And finally, as always, to my husband, Earl Georgas, proofreader par excellence!

Dear Reader,

*Welcome back to Our Canadian Girl!
In addition to this story about Angelique,
there are many more adventures of other
spirited girls to come.*

*So please keep on reading. And do stay
in touch. You can also log on to our website
at www.ourcanadiangirl.ca and enjoy fun
activities, sample chapters, a fan club, and
monthly contests.*

Sincerely,
 Barbara Berson
 Editor